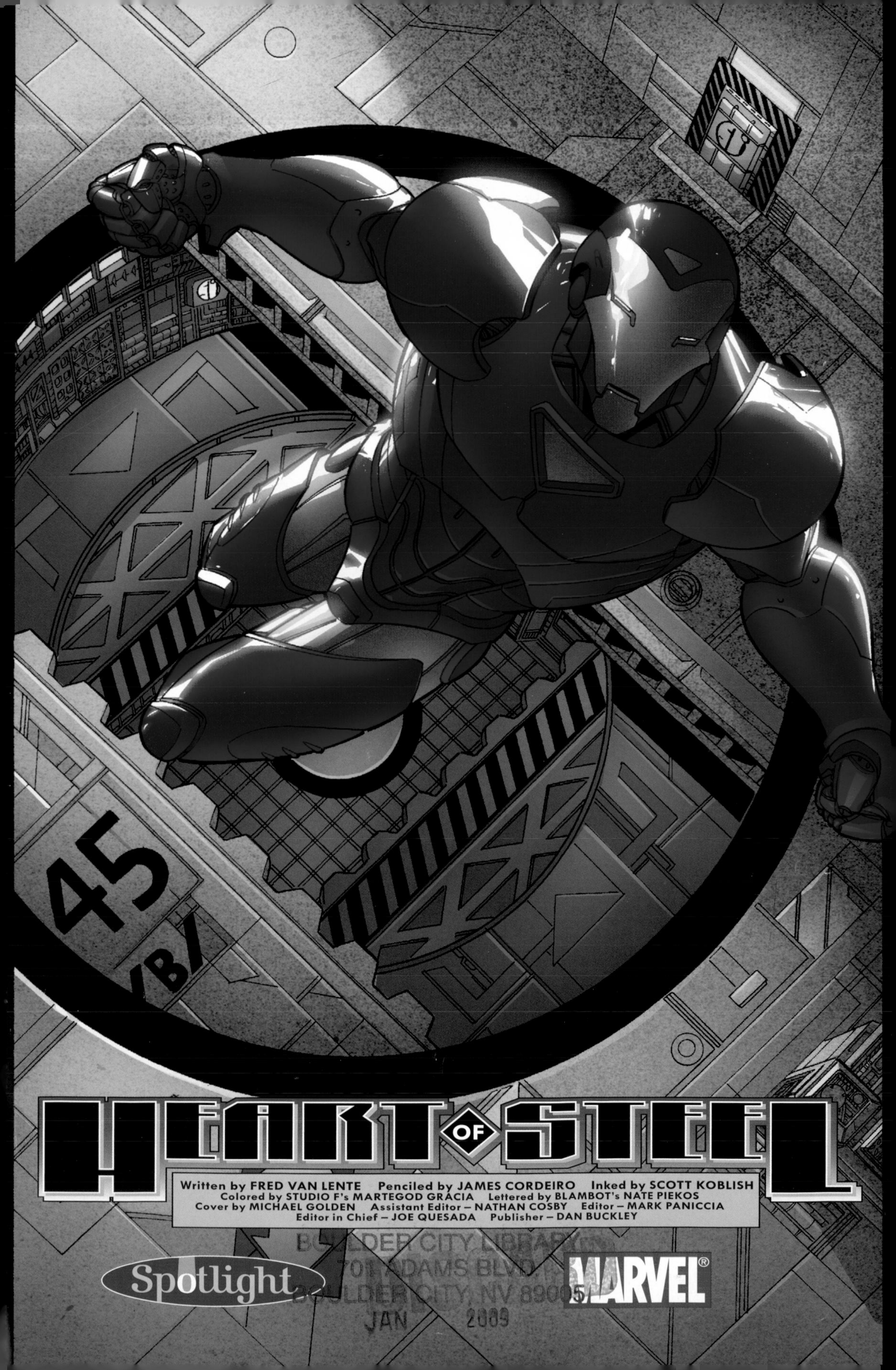
45
/B/
HEART OF STEEL
Written by FRED VAN LENTE Penciled by JAMES CORDEIRO Inked by SCOTT KOBLISH
Colored by STUDIO F's MARTEGOD GRACIA Lettered by BLAMBOT's NATE PIEKOS
Cover by MICHAEL GOLDEN Assistant Editor – NATHAN COSBY Editor – MARK PANICCIA
Editor in Chief – JOE QUESADA Publisher – DAN BUCKLEY
Spotlight
MARVEL®

VISIT US AT
www.abdopublishing.com

Reinforced library bound edition published in 2009 by Spotlight, a division of the ABDO
Publishing Group, 8000 West 78th Street, Edina, Minnesota 55439. Spotlight produces high-
quality reinforced library bound editions for schools and libraries. Published by agreement with
Marvel Characters, Inc.

Library of Congress Cataloging-in-Publication Data

Van Lente, Fred.
  Heart of steel / Fred Van Lente, writer ; James Cordeiro, penciler ; Scott Koblish, inker ;
Martegod Gracia, colorist ; Nate Piekos, letterer. -- Reinforced library bound ed.
     p. cm. -- (Iron Man)
  "Marvel."
  ISBN 978-1-59961-553-0
  1. Graphic novels. [1. Graphic novels.] I. Cordeiro, James, ill. II. Title.
  PZ7.7.V26Hec 2008
  [E]--dc22
                                        2008000104

All Spotlight books have reinforced library bindings and
are manufactured in the United States of America.

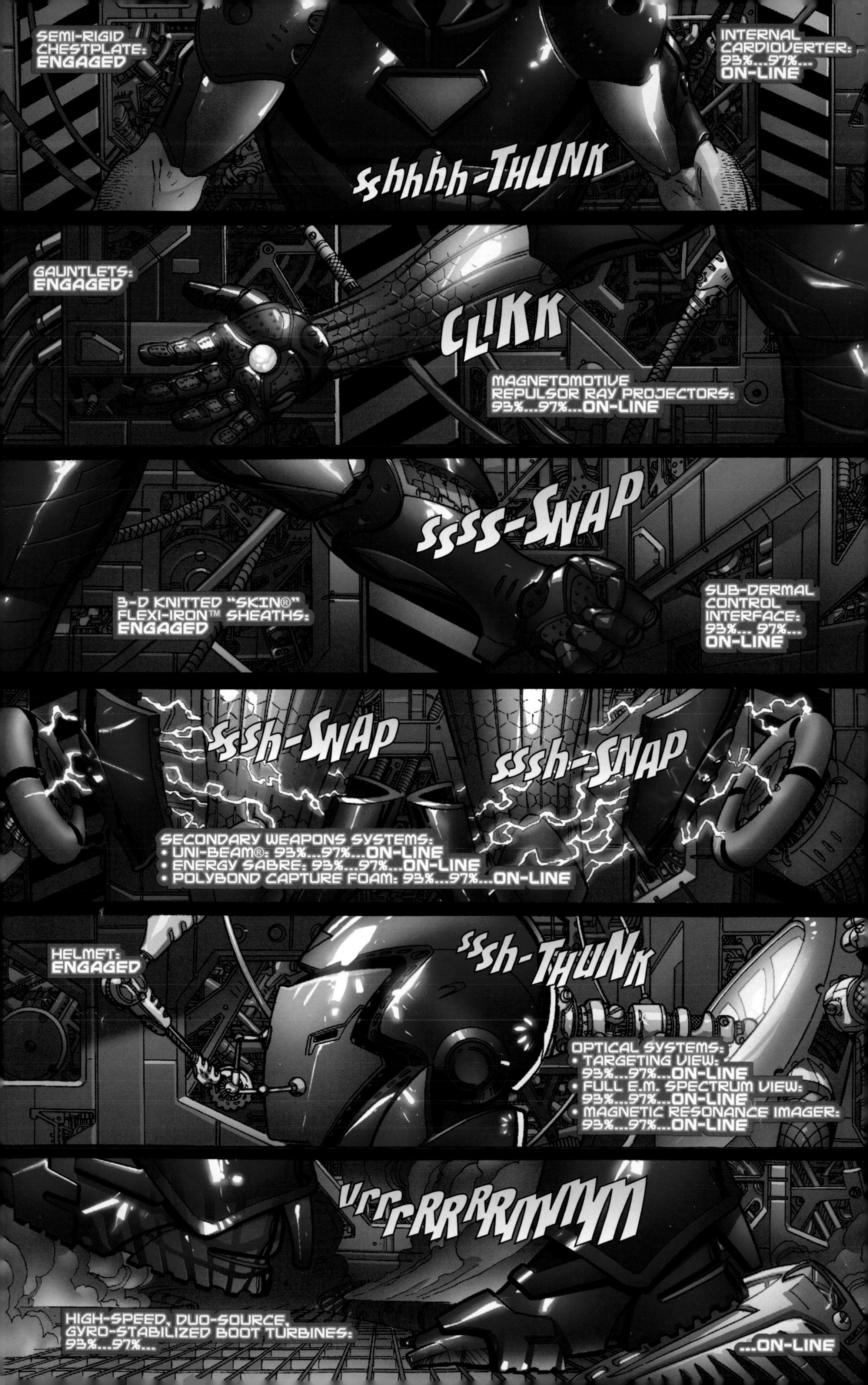
SEMI-RIGID CHESTPLATE: ENGAGED
INTERNAL CARDIOVERTER: 93%...97%... ON-LINE
SSHHHH-THUNK
GAUNTLETS: ENGAGED
CLIKK
MAGNETOMOTIVE REPULSOR RAY PROJECTORS: 93%...97%...ON-LINE
SSSS-SNAP
3-D KNITTED "SKIN®" FLEXI-IRON™ SHEATHS: ENGAGED
SUB-DERMAL CONTROL INTERFACE: 93%... 97%... ON-LINE
SSSH-SNAP
SSSH-SNAP
SECONDARY WEAPONS SYSTEMS:
• UNI-BEAM®: 93%...97%...ON-LINE
• ENERGY SABRE: 93%...97%...ON-LINE
• POLYBOND CAPTURE FOAM: 93%...97%...ON-LINE
HELMET: ENGAGED
SSSH-THUNK
OPTICAL SYSTEMS:
• TARGETING VIEW: 93%...97%...ON-LINE
• FULL E.M. SPECTRUM VIEW: 93%...97%...ON-LINE
• MAGNETIC RESONANCE IMAGER: 93%...97%...ON-LINE
VRRRRRRRMMM
HIGH-SPEED, DUO-SOURCE, GYRO-STABILIZED BOOT TURBINES: 93%...97%...
...ON-LINE

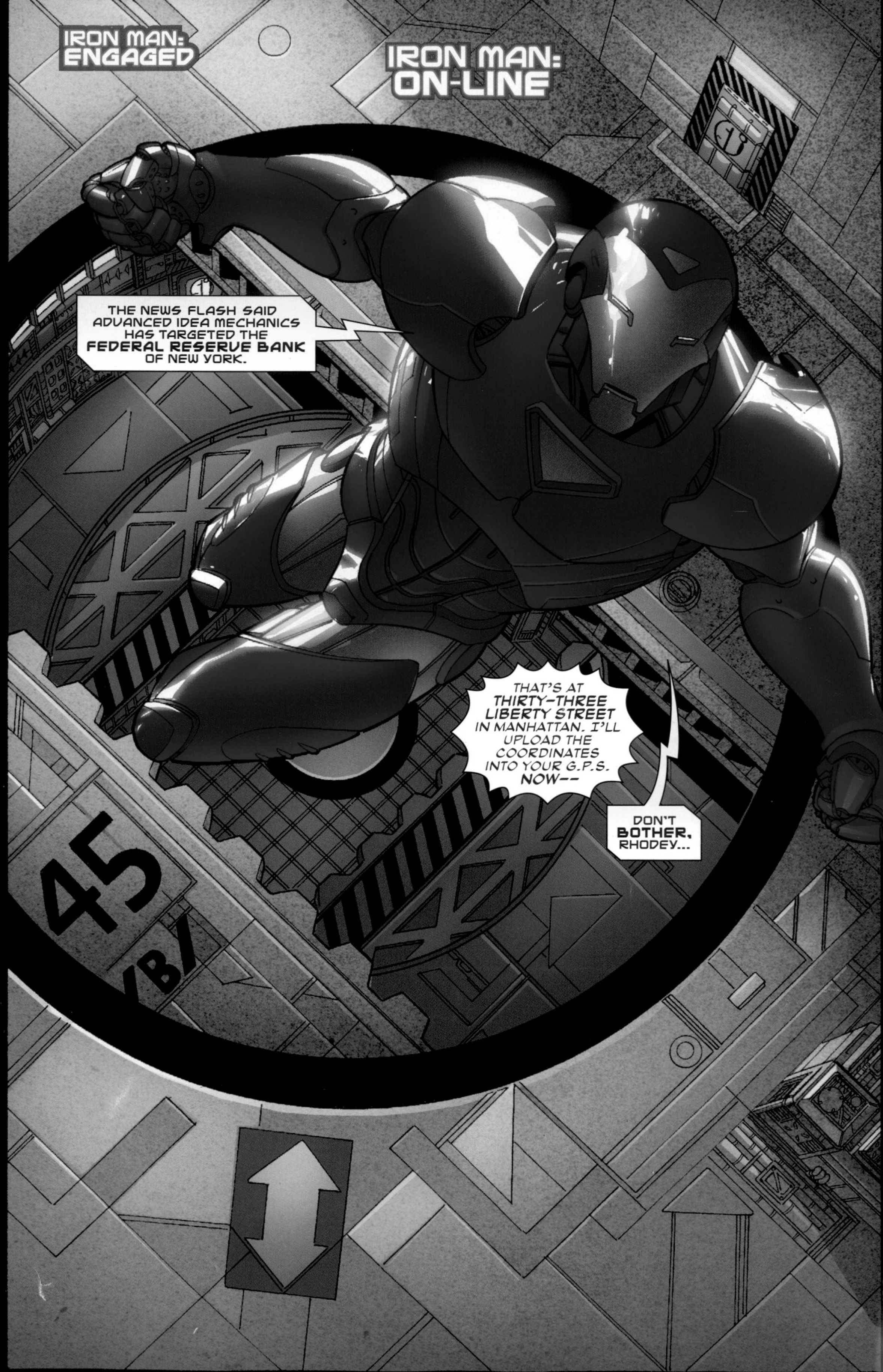
IRON MAN: ENGAGED
IRON MAN: ON-LINE
THE NEWS FLASH SAID ADVANCED IDEA MECHANICS HAS TARGETED THE FEDERAL RESERVE BANK OF NEW YORK.
THAT'S AT THIRTY-THREE LIBERTY STREET IN MANHATTAN. I'LL UPLOAD THE COORDINATES INTO YOUR G.P.S. NOW--
DON'T BOTHER, RHODEY...
45
/B/

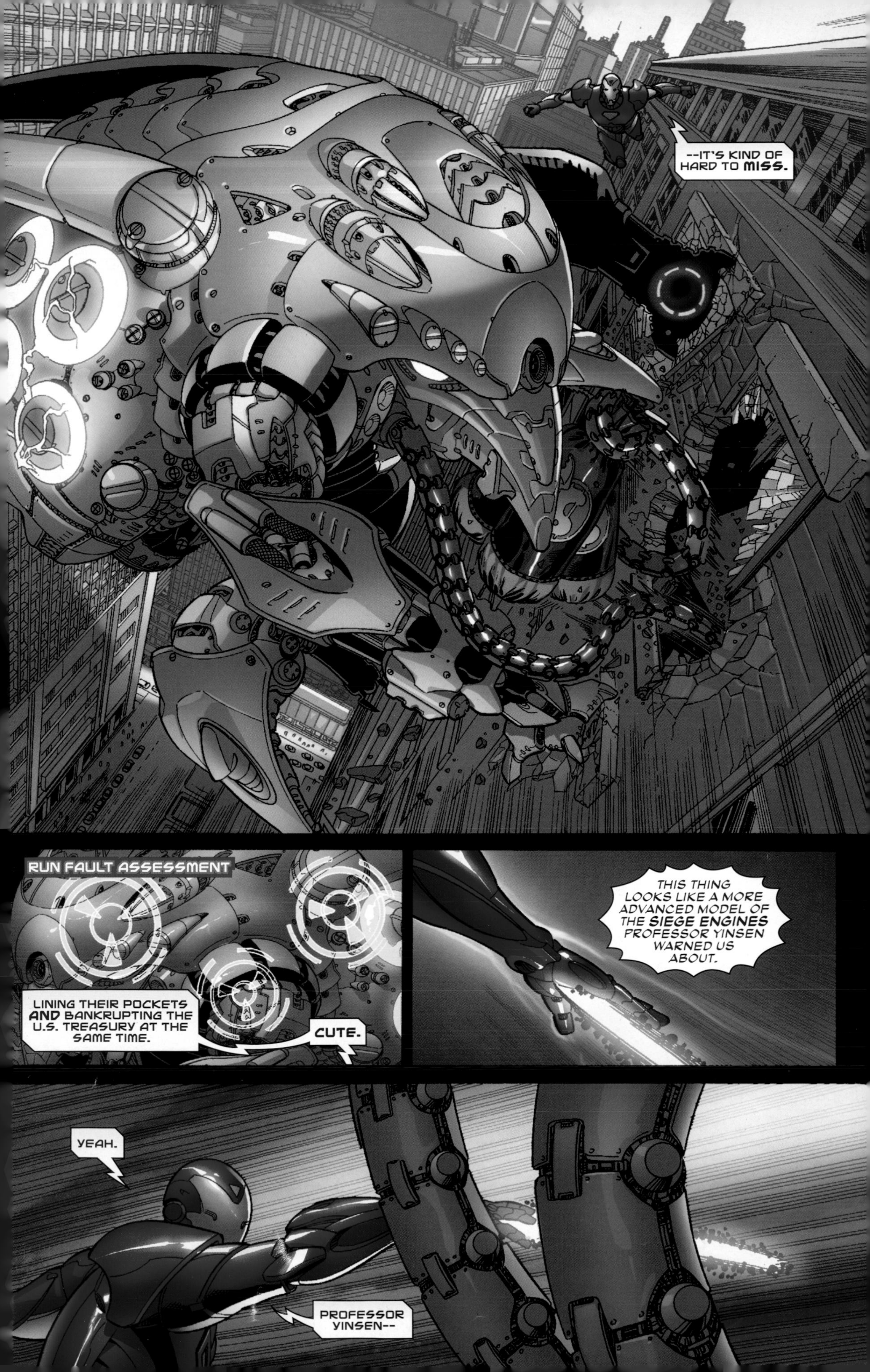
--IT'S KIND OF HARD TO MISS.
RUN FAULT ASSESSMENT
LINING THEIR POCKETS AND BANKRUPTING THE U.S. TREASURY AT THE SAME TIME.
CUTE.
THIS THING LOOKS LIKE A MORE ADVANCED MODEL OF THE SIEGE ENGINES PROFESSOR YINSEN WARNED US ABOUT.
YEAH.
PROFESSOR YINSEN--

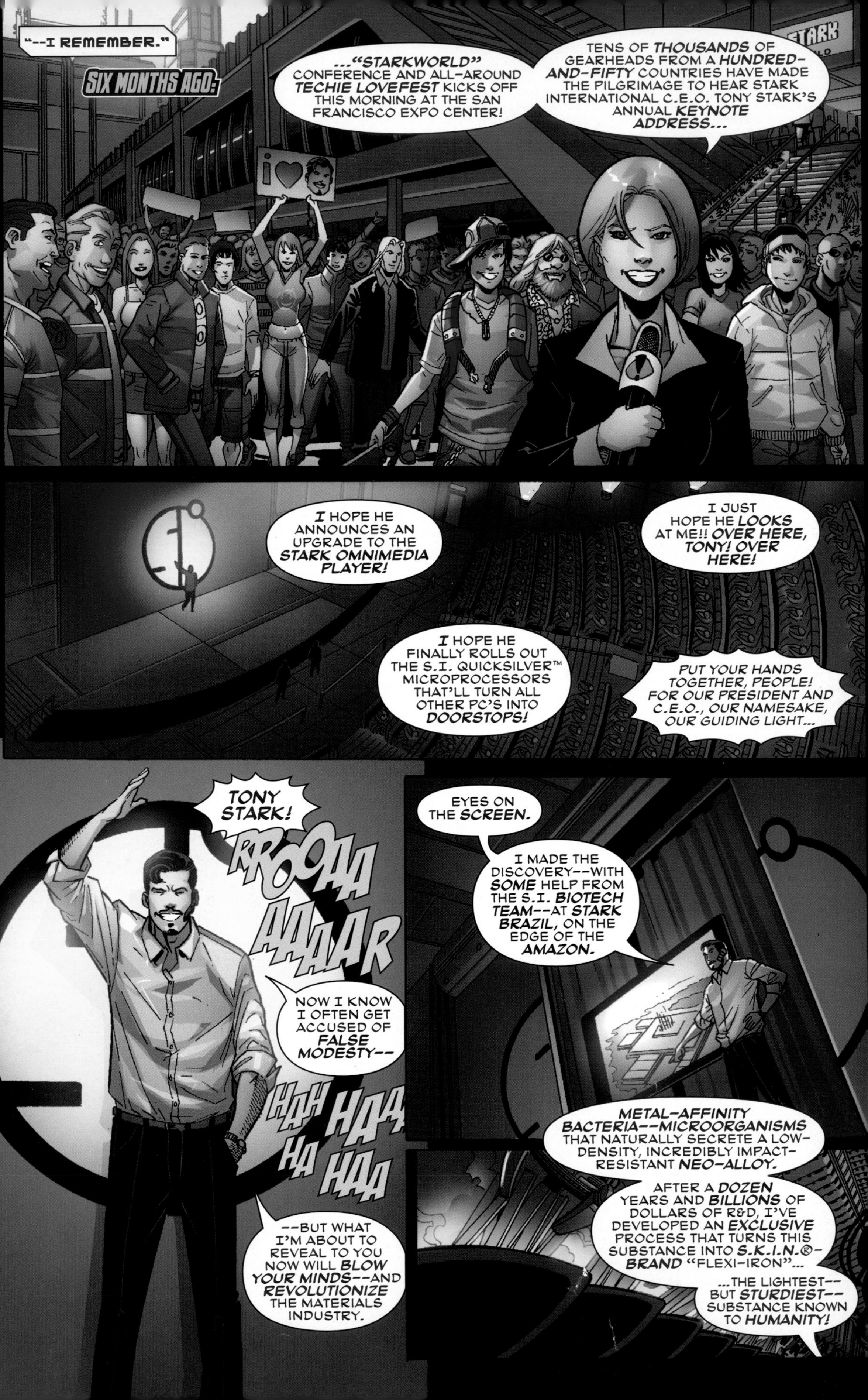
"--I REMEMBER."
SIX MONTHS AGO:
..."STARKWORLD" CONFERENCE AND ALL-AROUND TECHIE LOVEFEST KICKS OFF THIS MORNING AT THE SAN FRANCISCO EXPO CENTER!
TENS OF THOUSANDS OF GEARHEADS FROM A HUNDRED-AND-FIFTY COUNTRIES HAVE MADE THE PILGRIMAGE TO HEAR STARK INTERNATIONAL C.E.O. TONY STARK'S ANNUAL KEYNOTE ADDRESS...
I HOPE HE ANNOUNCES AN UPGRADE TO THE STARK OMNIMEDIA PLAYER!
I JUST HOPE HE LOOKS AT ME!! OVER HERE, TONY! OVER HERE!
I HOPE HE FINALLY ROLLS OUT THE S.I. QUICKSILVER™ MICROPROCESSORS THAT'LL TURN ALL OTHER PC'S INTO DOORSTOPS!
PUT YOUR HANDS TOGETHER, PEOPLE! FOR OUR PRESIDENT AND C.E.O., OUR NAMESAKE, OUR GUIDING LIGHT...
TONY STARK!
RROOAAAAAAR
NOW I KNOW I OFTEN GET ACCUSED OF FALSE MODESTY--
HAH HAA HA HAA
--BUT WHAT I'M ABOUT TO REVEAL TO YOU NOW WILL BLOW YOUR MINDS--AND REVOLUTIONIZE THE MATERIALS INDUSTRY.
EYES ON THE SCREEN.
I MADE THE DISCOVERY--WITH SOME HELP FROM THE S.I. BIOTECH TEAM--AT STARK BRAZIL, ON THE EDGE OF THE AMAZON.
METAL-AFFINITY BACTERIA--MICROORGANISMS THAT NATURALLY SECRETE A LOW-DENSITY, INCREDIBLY IMPACT-RESISTANT NEO-ALLOY.
AFTER A DOZEN YEARS AND BILLIONS OF DOLLARS OF R&D, I'VE DEVELOPED AN EXCLUSIVE PROCESS THAT TURNS THIS SUBSTANCE INTO S.K.I.N.®-BRAND "FLEXI-IRON"...
...THE LIGHTEST--BUT STURDIEST--SUBSTANCE KNOWN TO HUMANITY!

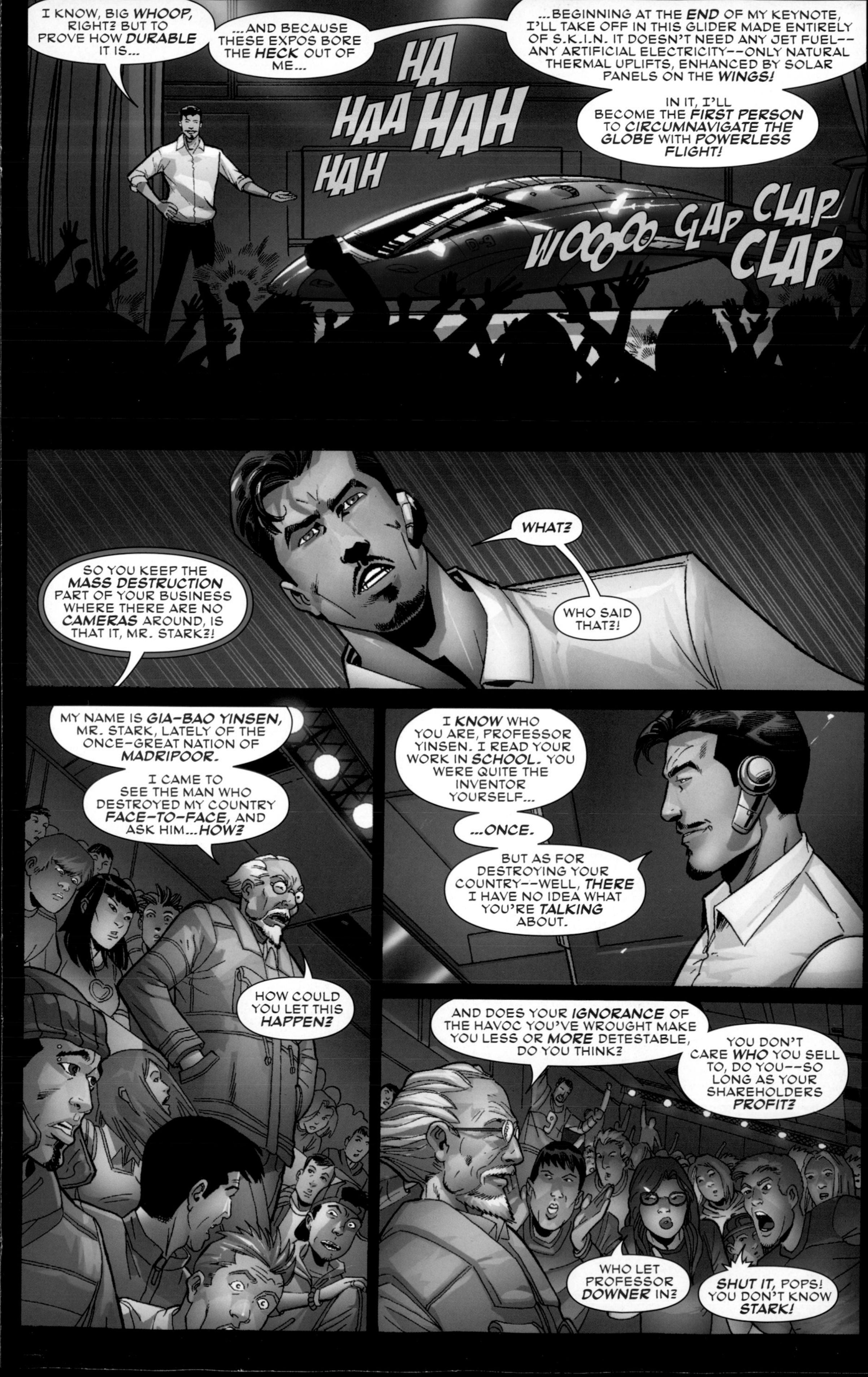
I KNOW, BIG WHOOP, RIGHT? BUT TO PROVE HOW DURABLE IT IS...
...AND BECAUSE THESE EXPOS BORE THE HECK OUT OF ME...
...BEGINNING AT THE END OF MY KEYNOTE, I'LL TAKE OFF IN THIS GLIDER MADE ENTIRELY OF S.K.I.N. IT DOESN'T NEED ANY JET FUEL--ANY ARTIFICIAL ELECTRICITY--ONLY NATURAL THERMAL UPLIFTS, ENHANCED BY SOLAR PANELS ON THE WINGS!
IN IT, I'LL BECOME THE FIRST PERSON TO CIRCUMNAVIGATE THE GLOBE WITH POWERLESS FLIGHT!
HA HAA HAH HAH
WOOOOO CLAP CLAP CLAP
WHAT?
SO YOU KEEP THE MASS DESTRUCTION PART OF YOUR BUSINESS WHERE THERE ARE NO CAMERAS AROUND, IS THAT IT, MR. STARK?!
WHO SAID THAT?!
MY NAME IS GIA-BAO YINSEN, MR. STARK, LATELY OF THE ONCE-GREAT NATION OF MADRIPOOR.
I CAME TO SEE THE MAN WHO DESTROYED MY COUNTRY FACE-TO-FACE, AND ASK HIM...HOW?
HOW COULD YOU LET THIS HAPPEN?
I KNOW WHO YOU ARE, PROFESSOR YINSEN. I READ YOUR WORK IN SCHOOL. YOU WERE QUITE THE INVENTOR YOURSELF...
...ONCE.
BUT AS FOR DESTROYING YOUR COUNTRY--WELL, THERE I HAVE NO IDEA WHAT YOU'RE TALKING ABOUT.
AND DOES YOUR IGNORANCE OF THE HAVOC YOU'VE WROUGHT MAKE YOU LESS OR MORE DETESTABLE, DO YOU THINK?
YOU DON'T CARE WHO YOU SELL TO, DO YOU--SO LONG AS YOUR SHAREHOLDERS PROFIT?
WHO LET PROFESSOR DOWNER IN?
SHUT IT, POPS! YOU DON'T KNOW STARK!

"ADVANCED IDEA MECHANICS TERRORISTS HAVE TAKEN YOUR UNI-BEAM AND HOVER PLATFORMS... COMBINED THEM INTO SIEGE ENGINES THAT ARE LAYING WASTE TO MADRIPOOR EVEN AS WE SPEAK!

"OUR GOVERNMENT IS NEAR COLLAPSE-- ALL BECAUSE OF YOU AND YOUR MACHINES! AND NO ONE IN THE WEST SEEMS TO CARE!"

BITTER OLD FAILURE... TRYING TO RUIN STARKWORLD!

ANY WAY YOU CAN USE YOUR OLD SERVICE CONNECTIONS, RHODEY, FIND OUT IF THERE'S ANY TRUTH TO HIS RANTING?

THERE'S CALLS I CAN MAKE. BUT I'M SURE THE GEEZER'S JUST ANOTHER CRACKPOT, TONE.

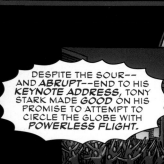

C'MON, GRANDPA, THE EXIT'S THIS WAY...

...FOR YOUR OWN HEALTH I SUGGEST YOU USE IT.

WAIT-- AREN'T YOU GOING TO FINISH YOUR ADDRESS, BOSS?

NOT NOW, PEPPER--

I'M NOT IN THE MOOD.

DESPITE THE SOUR-- AND ABRUPT--END TO HIS KEYNOTE ADDRESS, TONY STARK MADE GOOD ON HIS PROMISE TO ATTEMPT TO CIRCLE THE GLOBE WITH POWERLESS FLIGHT.

NOT SINCE THE DAYS OF CHARLES LINDBERGH AND THE SPIRIT OF ST. LOUIS HAS AN AERONAUTICAL FEAT BEEN ANTICIPATED WITH SUCH EXCITEMENT...

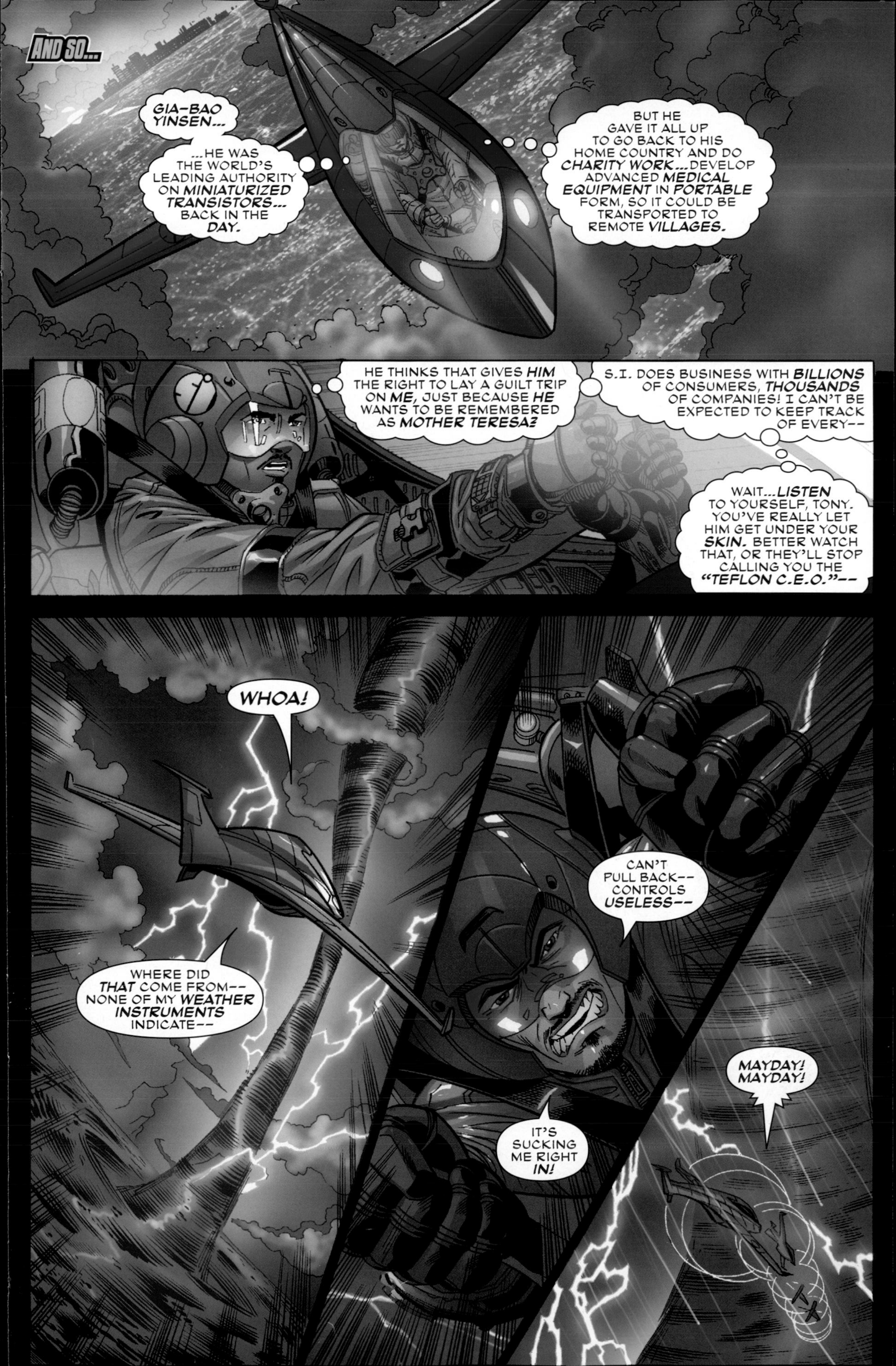
AND SO...
GIA-BAO YINSEN...
...HE WAS THE WORLD'S LEADING AUTHORITY ON MINIATURIZED TRANSISTORS... BACK IN THE DAY.
BUT HE GAVE IT ALL UP TO GO BACK TO HIS HOME COUNTRY AND DO CHARITY WORK...DEVELOP ADVANCED MEDICAL EQUIPMENT IN PORTABLE FORM, SO IT COULD BE TRANSPORTED TO REMOTE VILLAGES.
HE THINKS THAT GIVES HIM THE RIGHT TO LAY A GUILT TRIP ON ME, JUST BECAUSE HE WANTS TO BE REMEMBERED AS MOTHER TERESA?
S.I. DOES BUSINESS WITH BILLIONS OF CONSUMERS, THOUSANDS OF COMPANIES! I CAN'T BE EXPECTED TO KEEP TRACK OF EVERY--
WAIT...LISTEN TO YOURSELF, TONY. YOU'VE REALLY LET HIM GET UNDER YOUR SKIN. BETTER WATCH THAT, OR THEY'LL STOP CALLING YOU THE "TEFLON C.E.O."--
WHOA!
WHERE DID THAT COME FROM-- NONE OF MY WEATHER INSTRUMENTS INDICATE--
CAN'T PULL BACK-- CONTROLS USELESS--
IT'S SUCKING ME RIGHT IN!
MAYDAY! MAYDAY!

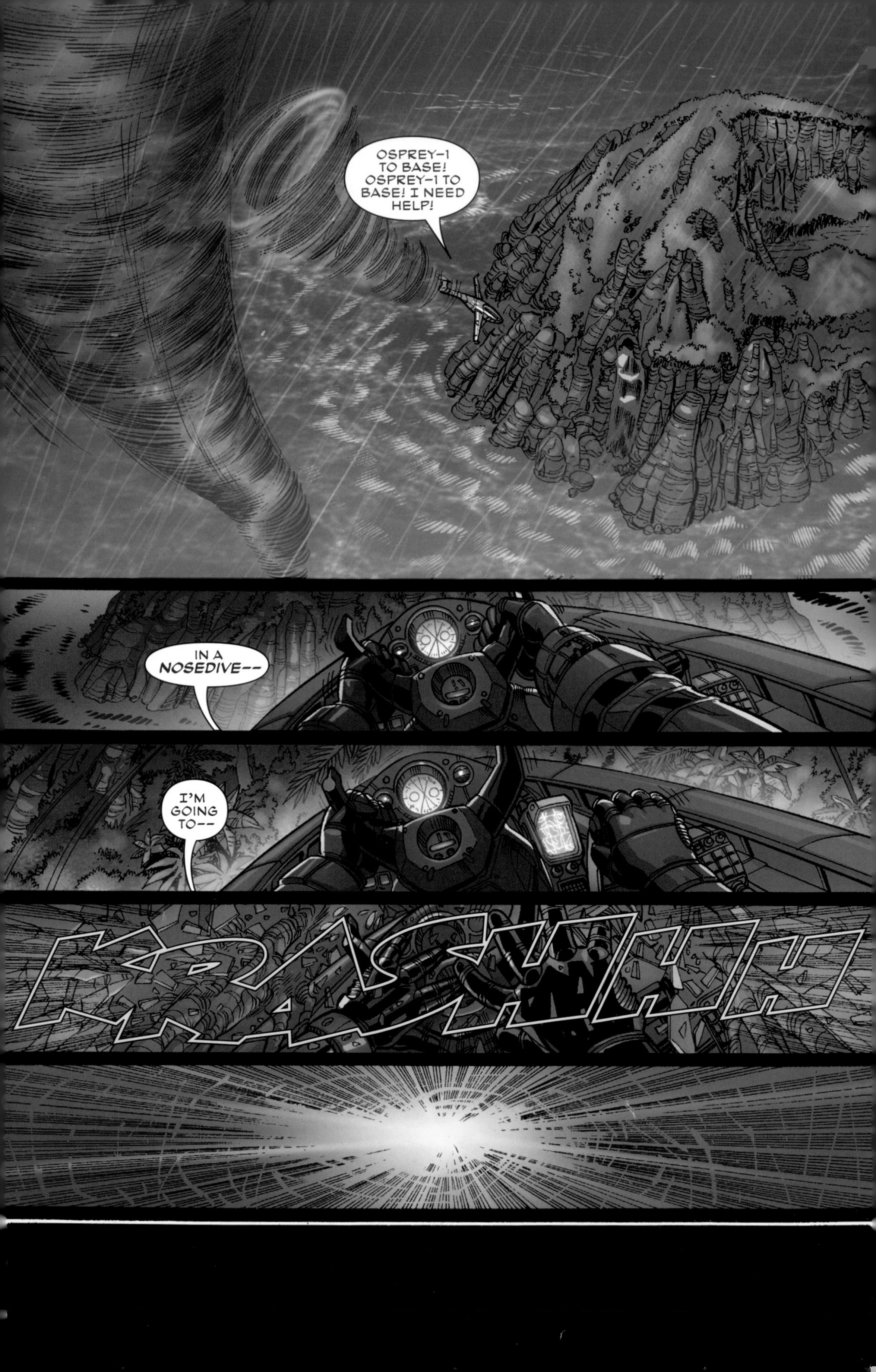
OSPREY-1 TO BASE! OSPREY-1 TO BASE! I NEED HELP!
IN A NOSEDIVE--
I'M GOING TO--
KRASHHH

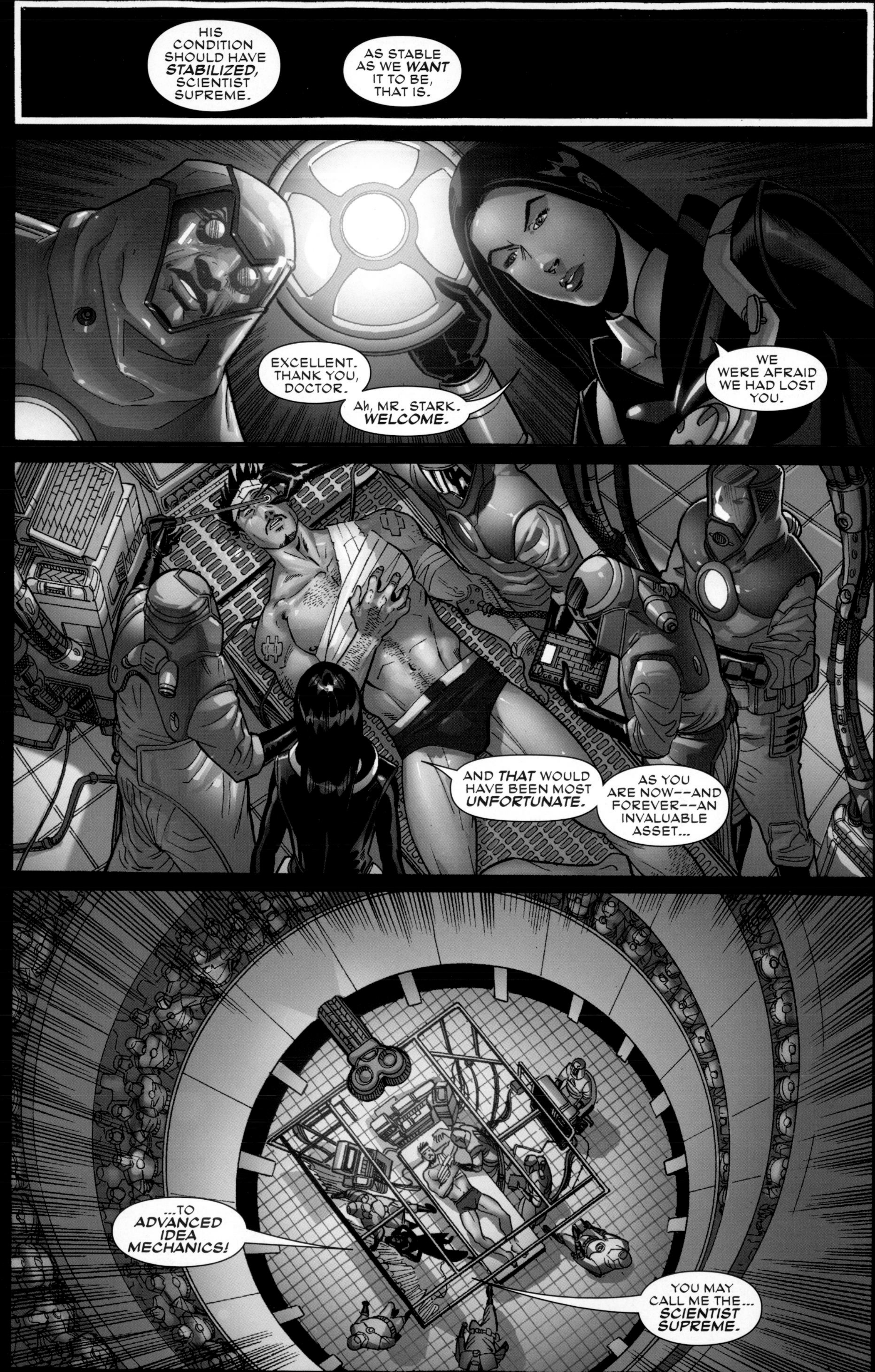
HIS CONDITION SHOULD HAVE STABILIZED, SCIENTIST SUPREME.
AS STABLE AS WE WANT IT TO BE, THAT IS.
EXCELLENT. THANK YOU, DOCTOR.
Ah, MR. STARK. WELCOME.
WE WERE AFRAID WE HAD LOST YOU.
AND THAT WOULD HAVE BEEN MOST UNFORTUNATE.
AS YOU ARE NOW--AND FOREVER--AN INVALUABLE ASSET...
...TO ADVANCED IDEA MECHANICS!
YOU MAY CALL ME THE... SCIENTIST SUPREME.

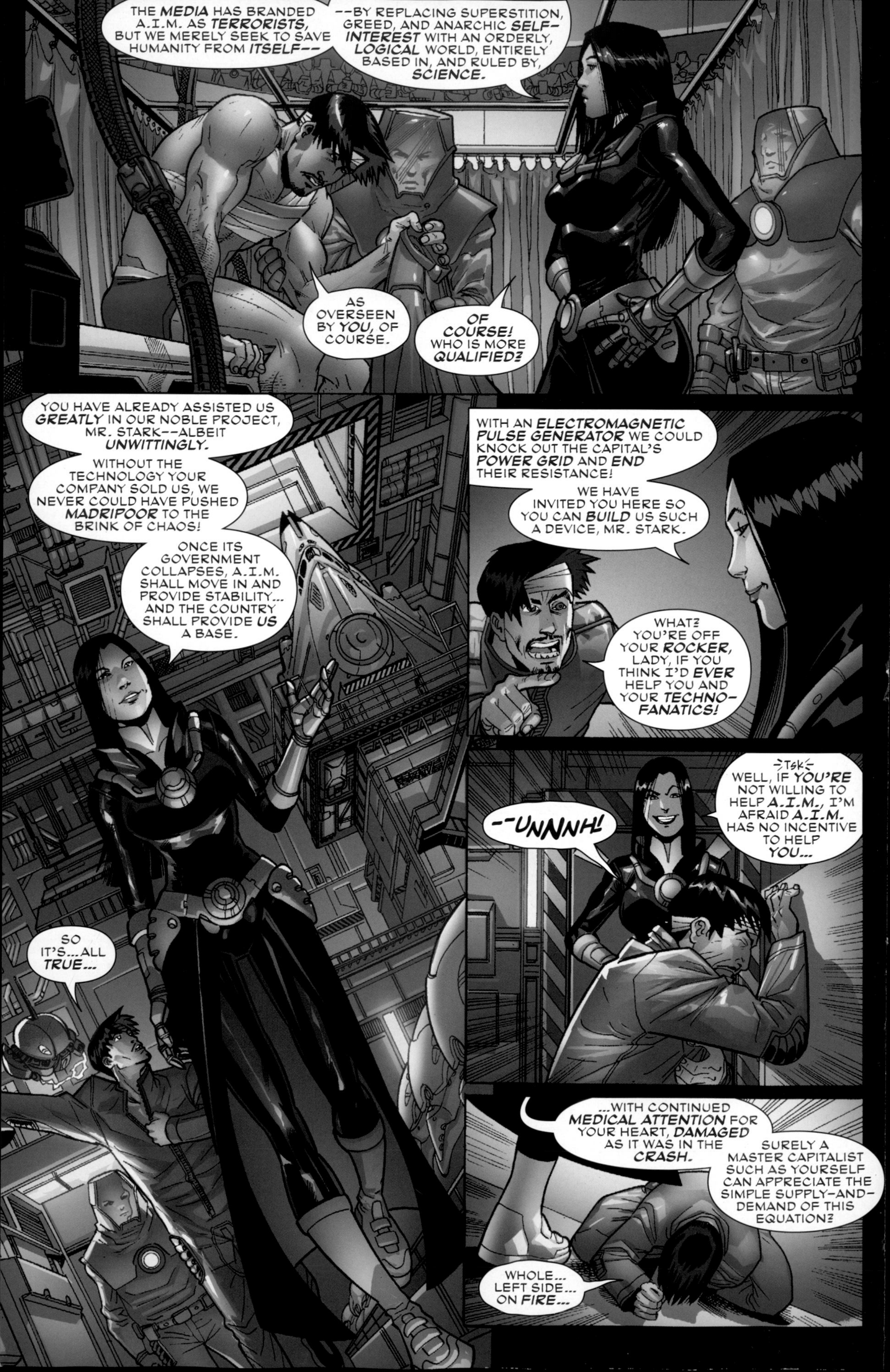

THE MEDIA HAS BRANDED A.I.M. AS TERRORISTS, BUT WE MERELY SEEK TO SAVE HUMANITY FROM ITSELF--
--BY REPLACING SUPERSTITION, GREED, AND ANARCHIC SELF-INTEREST WITH AN ORDERLY, LOGICAL WORLD, ENTIRELY BASED IN, AND RULED BY, SCIENCE.
AS OVERSEEN BY YOU, OF COURSE.
OF COURSE! WHO IS MORE QUALIFIED?
YOU HAVE ALREADY ASSISTED US GREATLY IN OUR NOBLE PROJECT, MR. STARK--ALBEIT UNWITTINGLY.
WITHOUT THE TECHNOLOGY YOUR COMPANY SOLD US, WE NEVER COULD HAVE PUSHED MADRIPOOR TO THE BRINK OF CHAOS!
ONCE ITS GOVERNMENT COLLAPSES, A.I.M. SHALL MOVE IN AND PROVIDE STABILITY... AND THE COUNTRY SHALL PROVIDE US A BASE.
SO IT'S...ALL TRUE...
WITH AN ELECTROMAGNETIC PULSE GENERATOR WE COULD KNOCK OUT THE CAPITAL'S POWER GRID AND END THEIR RESISTANCE!
WE HAVE INVITED YOU HERE SO YOU CAN BUILD US SUCH A DEVICE, MR. STARK.
WHAT? YOU'RE OFF YOUR ROCKER, LADY, IF YOU THINK I'D EVER HELP YOU AND YOUR TECHNO-FANATICS!
--UNNNH!
TSK
WELL, IF YOU'RE NOT WILLING TO HELP A.I.M., I'M AFRAID A.I.M. HAS NO INCENTIVE TO HELP YOU...
...WITH CONTINUED MEDICAL ATTENTION FOR YOUR HEART, DAMAGED AS IT WAS IN THE CRASH.
SURELY A MASTER CAPITALIST SUCH AS YOURSELF CAN APPRECIATE THE SIMPLE SUPPLY-AND-DEMAND OF THIS EQUATION?
WHOLE... LEFT SIDE... ON FIRE...

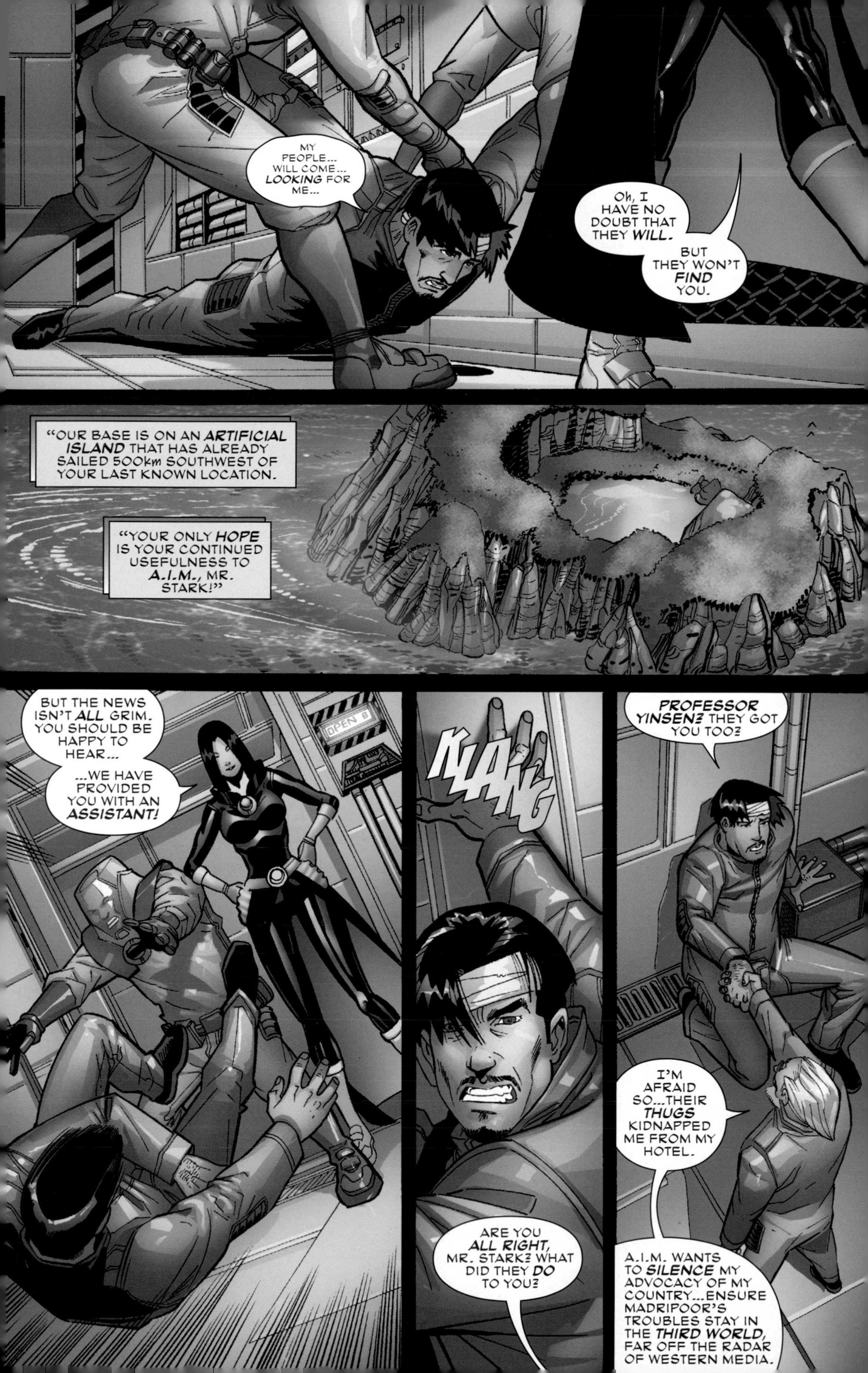
MY PEOPLE... WILL COME... LOOKING FOR ME...
Oh, I HAVE NO DOUBT THAT THEY WILL.
BUT THEY WON'T FIND YOU.
"OUR BASE IS ON AN ARTIFICIAL ISLAND THAT HAS ALREADY SAILED 500km SOUTHWEST OF YOUR LAST KNOWN LOCATION.
"YOUR ONLY HOPE IS YOUR CONTINUED USEFULNESS TO A.I.M., MR. STARK!"
BUT THE NEWS ISN'T ALL GRIM. YOU SHOULD BE HAPPY TO HEAR...
...WE HAVE PROVIDED YOU WITH AN ASSISTANT!
OPEN
KLANG
ARE YOU ALL RIGHT, MR. STARK? WHAT DID THEY DO TO YOU?
PROFESSOR YINSEN? THEY GOT YOU TOO?
I'M AFRAID SO...THEIR THUGS KIDNAPPED ME FROM MY HOTEL.
A.I.M. WANTS TO SILENCE MY ADVOCACY OF MY COUNTRY...ENSURE MADRIPOOR'S TROUBLES STAY IN THE THIRD WORLD, FAR OFF THE RADAR OF WESTERN MEDIA.

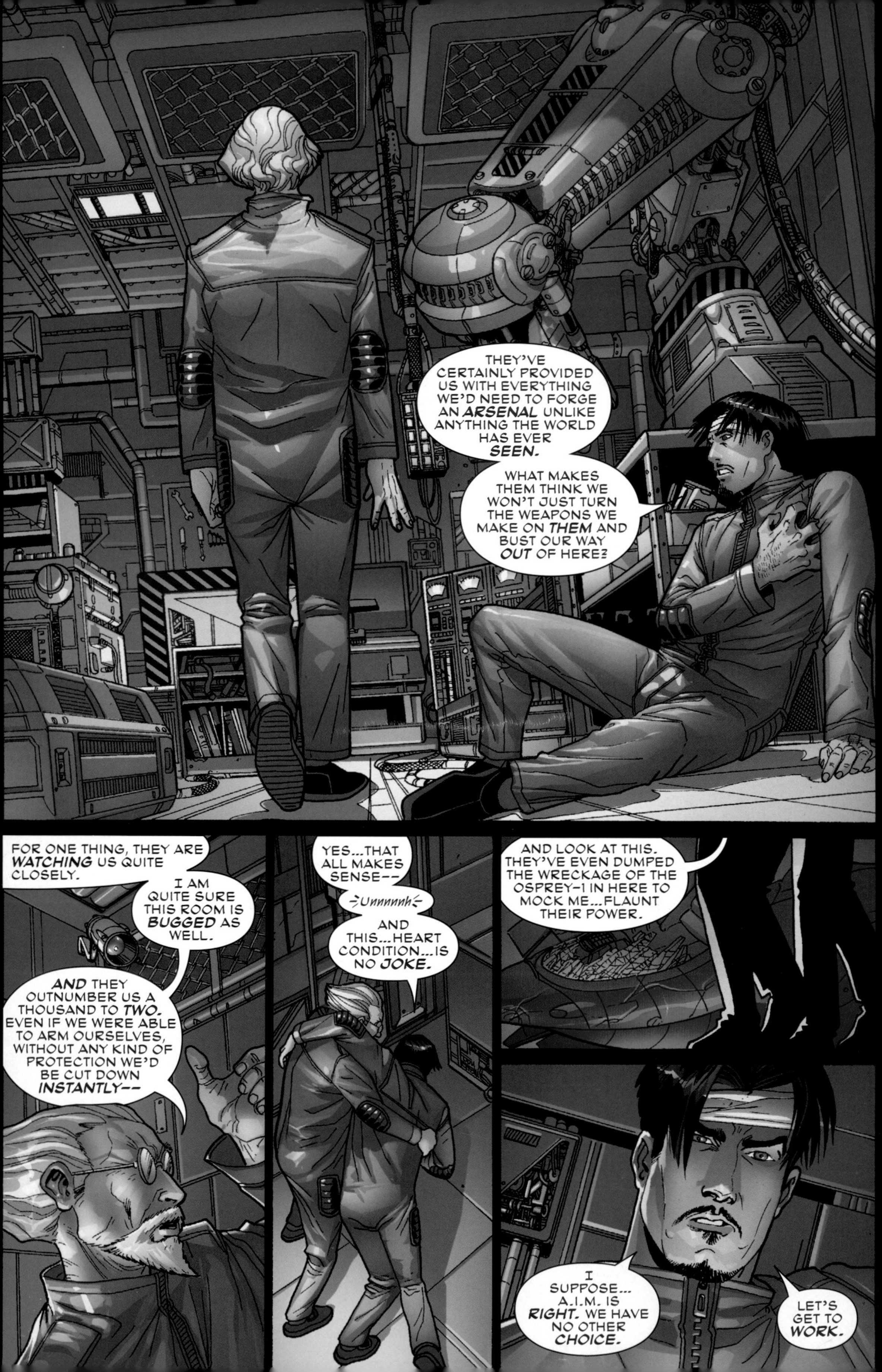
THEY'VE CERTAINLY PROVIDED US WITH EVERYTHING WE'D NEED TO FORGE AN ARSENAL UNLIKE ANYTHING THE WORLD HAS EVER SEEN.
WHAT MAKES THEM THINK WE WON'T JUST TURN THE WEAPONS WE MAKE ON THEM AND BUST OUR WAY OUT OF HERE?
FOR ONE THING, THEY ARE WATCHING US QUITE CLOSELY.
I AM QUITE SURE THIS ROOM IS BUGGED AS WELL.
AND THEY OUTNUMBER US A THOUSAND TO TWO. EVEN IF WE WERE ABLE TO ARM OURSELVES, WITHOUT ANY KIND OF PROTECTION WE'D BE CUT DOWN INSTANTLY--
YES...THAT ALL MAKES SENSE--
Unnnnnh
AND THIS...HEART CONDITION...IS NO JOKE.
AND LOOK AT THIS. THEY'VE EVEN DUMPED THE WRECKAGE OF THE OSPREY-1 IN HERE TO MOCK ME...FLAUNT THEIR POWER.
I SUPPOSE... A.I.M. IS RIGHT. WE HAVE NO OTHER CHOICE.
LET'S GET TO WORK.

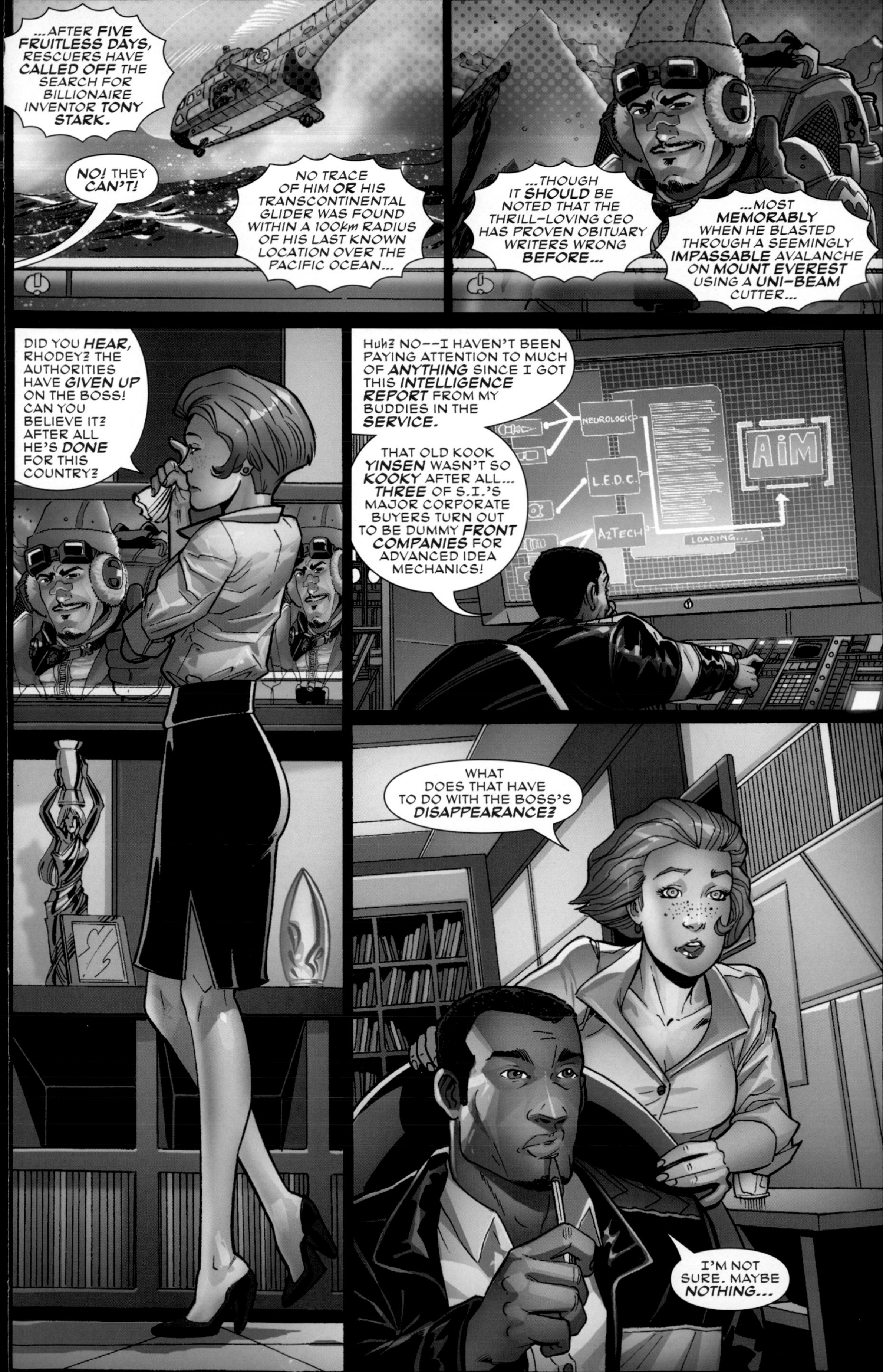
...AFTER FIVE FRUITLESS DAYS, RESCUERS HAVE CALLED OFF THE SEARCH FOR BILLIONAIRE INVENTOR TONY STARK.
NO! THEY CAN'T!
NO TRACE OF HIM OR HIS TRANSCONTINENTAL GLIDER WAS FOUND WITHIN A 100km RADIUS OF HIS LAST KNOWN LOCATION OVER THE PACIFIC OCEAN...
...THOUGH IT SHOULD BE NOTED THAT THE THRILL-LOVING CEO HAS PROVEN OBITUARY WRITERS WRONG BEFORE...
...MOST MEMORABLY WHEN HE BLASTED THROUGH A SEEMINGLY IMPASSABLE AVALANCHE ON MOUNT EVEREST USING A UNI-BEAM CUTTER...
DID YOU HEAR, RHODEY? THE AUTHORITIES HAVE GIVEN UP ON THE BOSS! CAN YOU BELIEVE IT? AFTER ALL HE'S DONE FOR THIS COUNTRY?
Huh? NO--I HAVEN'T BEEN PAYING ATTENTION TO MUCH OF ANYTHING SINCE I GOT THIS INTELLIGENCE REPORT FROM MY BUDDIES IN THE SERVICE.
THAT OLD KOOK YINSEN WASN'T SO KOOKY AFTER ALL... THREE OF S.I.'S MAJOR CORPORATE BUYERS TURN OUT TO BE DUMMY FRONT COMPANIES FOR ADVANCED IDEA MECHANICS!
NEUROLOGIC
L.E.D.C.
AzTECH
AiM
LOADING...
WHAT DOES THAT HAVE TO DO WITH THE BOSS'S DISAPPEARANCE?
I'M NOT SURE. MAYBE NOTHING...

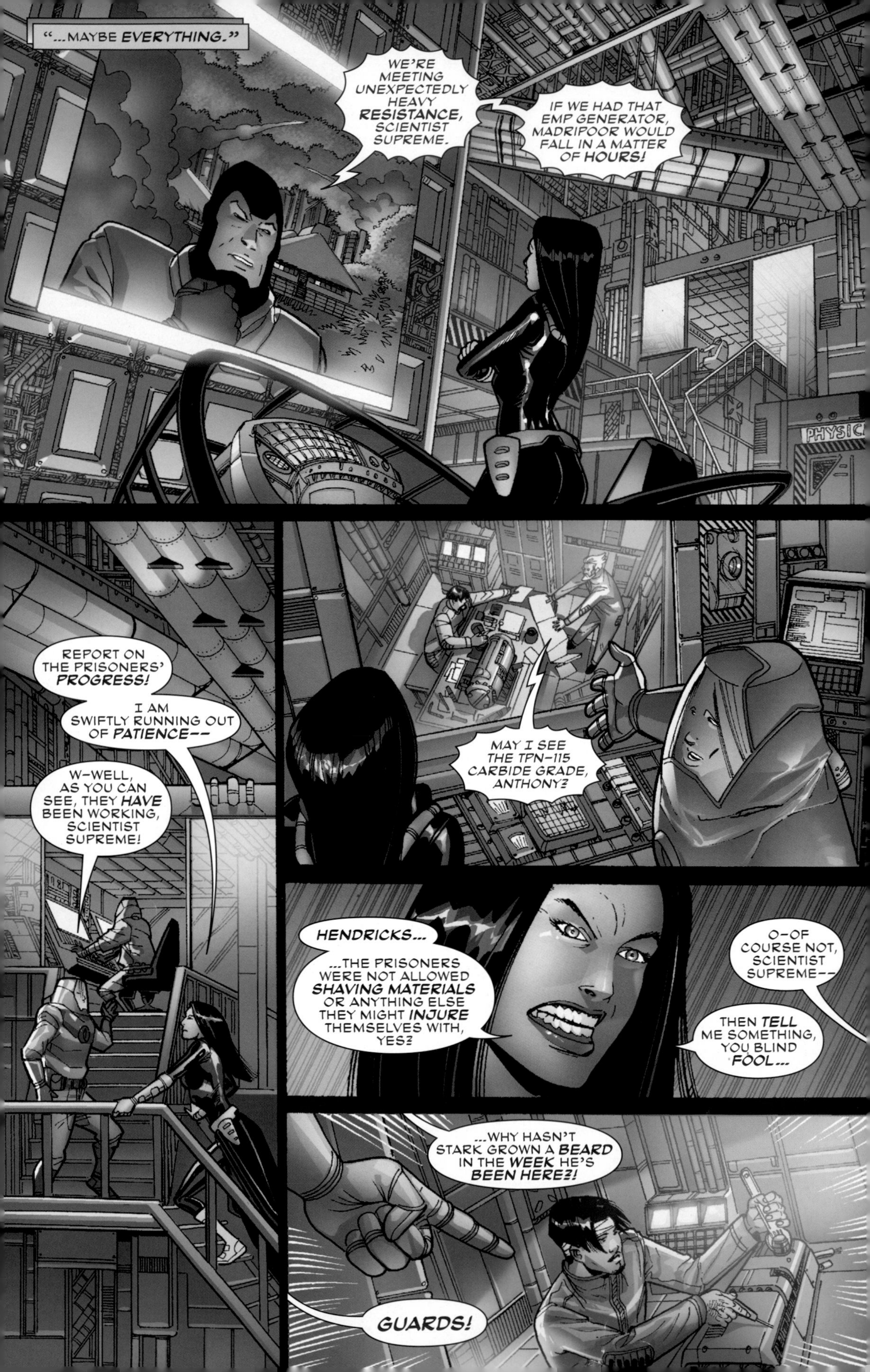
"...MAYBE EVERYTHING."
WE'RE MEETING UNEXPECTEDLY HEAVY RESISTANCE, SCIENTIST SUPREME.
IF WE HAD THAT EMP GENERATOR, MADRIPOOR WOULD FALL IN A MATTER OF HOURS!
PHYSIC
REPORT ON THE PRISONERS' PROGRESS!
I AM SWIFTLY RUNNING OUT OF PATIENCE--
W-WELL, AS YOU CAN SEE, THEY HAVE BEEN WORKING, SCIENTIST SUPREME!
MAY I SEE THE TPN-115 CARBIDE GRADE, ANTHONY?
HENDRICKS...
...THE PRISONERS WERE NOT ALLOWED SHAVING MATERIALS OR ANYTHING ELSE THEY MIGHT INJURE THEMSELVES WITH, YES?
O-OF COURSE NOT, SCIENTIST SUPREME--
THEN TELL ME SOMETHING, YOU BLIND FOOL...
...WHY HASN'T STARK GROWN A BEARD IN THE WEEK HE'S BEEN HERE?!
GUARDS!

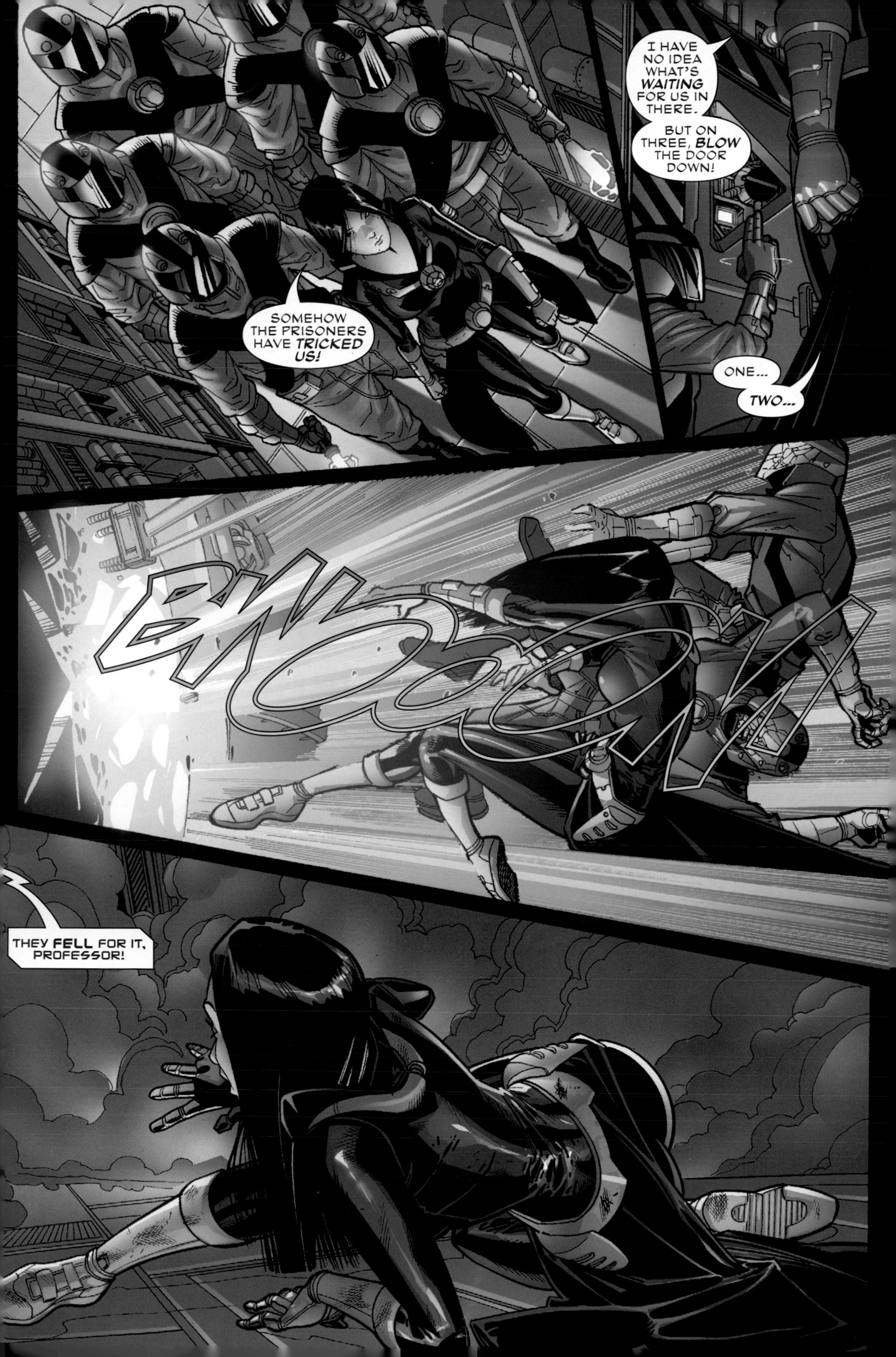

SOMEHOW THE PRISONERS HAVE TRICKED US!
I HAVE NO IDEA WHAT'S WAITING FOR US IN THERE.
BUT ON THREE, BLOW THE DOOR DOWN!
ONE...
TWO...
THEY FELL FOR IT, PROFESSOR!

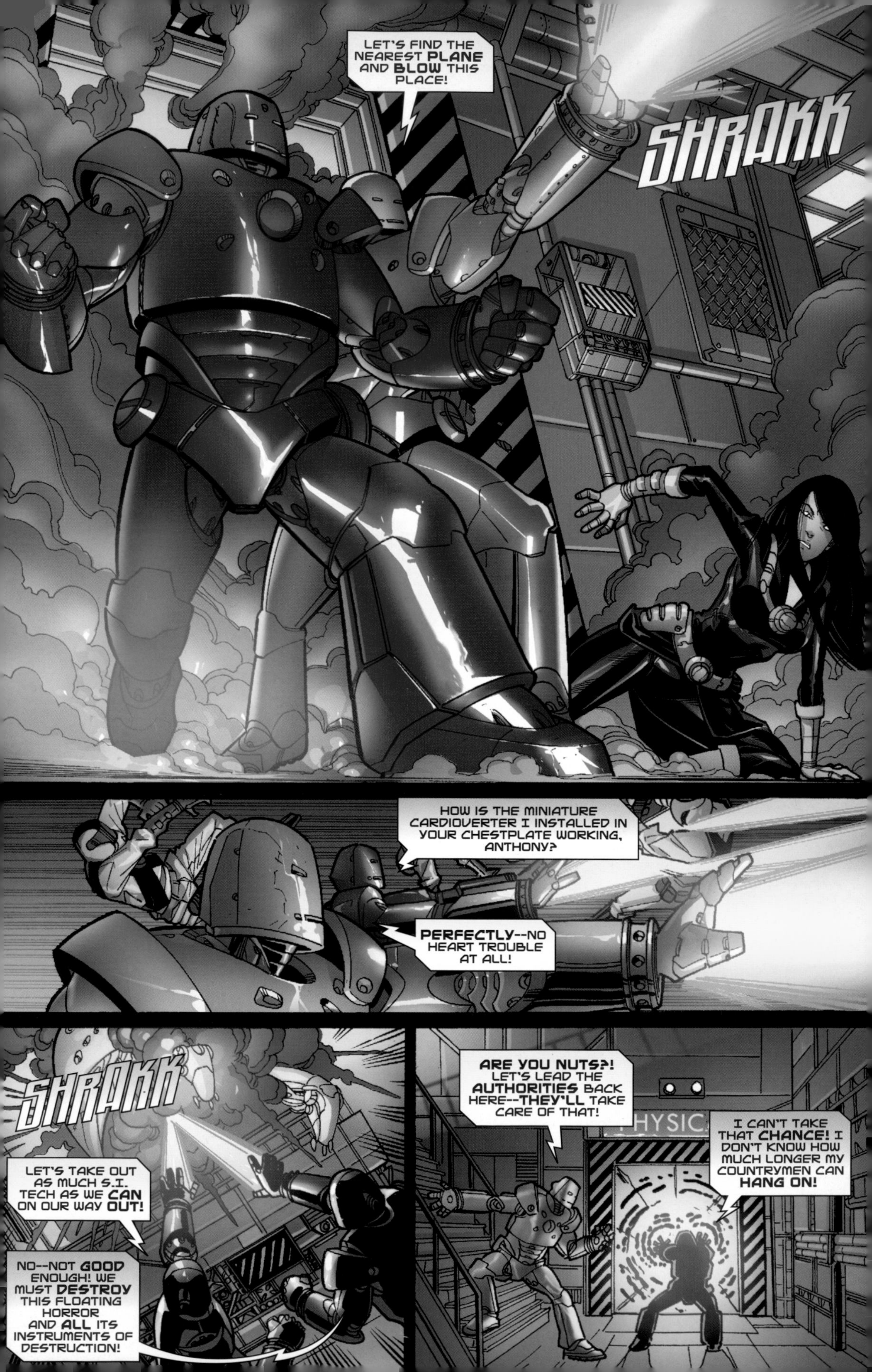
LET'S FIND THE NEAREST PLANE AND BLOW THIS PLACE!
SHRAKK
HOW IS THE MINIATURE CARDIOVERTER I INSTALLED IN YOUR CHESTPLATE WORKING, ANTHONY?
PERFECTLY--NO HEART TROUBLE AT ALL!
SHRAKK
LET'S TAKE OUT AS MUCH S.I. TECH AS WE CAN ON OUR WAY OUT!
NO--NOT GOOD ENOUGH! WE MUST DESTROY THIS FLOATING HORROR AND ALL ITS INSTRUMENTS OF DESTRUCTION!
ARE YOU NUTS?! LET'S LEAD THE AUTHORITIES BACK HERE--THEY'LL TAKE CARE OF THAT!
I CAN'T TAKE THAT CHANCE! I DON'T KNOW HOW MUCH LONGER MY COUNTRYMEN CAN HANG ON!

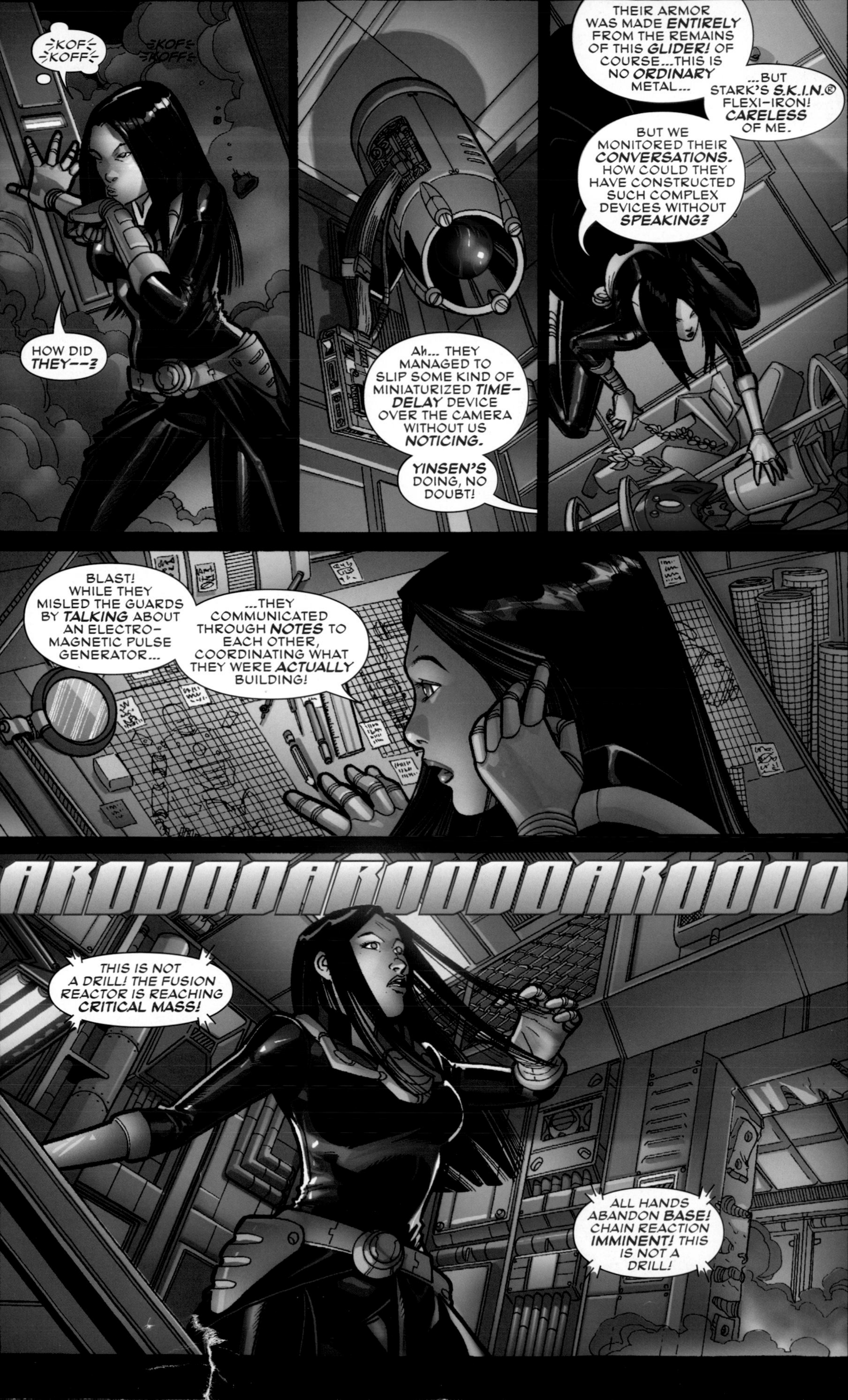
KOF KOFF
KOF KOFF
HOW DID THEY--?
Ah... THEY MANAGED TO SLIP SOME KIND OF MINIATURIZED TIME-DELAY DEVICE OVER THE CAMERA WITHOUT US NOTICING.
YINSEN'S DOING, NO DOUBT!
THEIR ARMOR WAS MADE ENTIRELY FROM THE REMAINS OF THIS GLIDER! OF COURSE...THIS IS NO ORDINARY METAL...
...BUT STARK'S S.K.I.N.® FLEXI-IRON! CARELESS OF ME.
BUT WE MONITORED THEIR CONVERSATIONS. HOW COULD THEY HAVE CONSTRUCTED SUCH COMPLEX DEVICES WITHOUT SPEAKING?
BLAST! WHILE THEY MISLED THE GUARDS BY TALKING ABOUT AN ELECTRO-MAGNETIC PULSE GENERATOR...
...THEY COMMUNICATED THROUGH NOTES TO EACH OTHER, COORDINATING WHAT THEY WERE ACTUALLY BUILDING!
AROOOOAROOOOAROOOO
THIS IS NOT A DRILL! THE FUSION REACTOR IS REACHING CRITICAL MASS!
ALL HANDS ABANDON BASE! CHAIN REACTION IMMINENT! THIS IS NOT A DRILL!

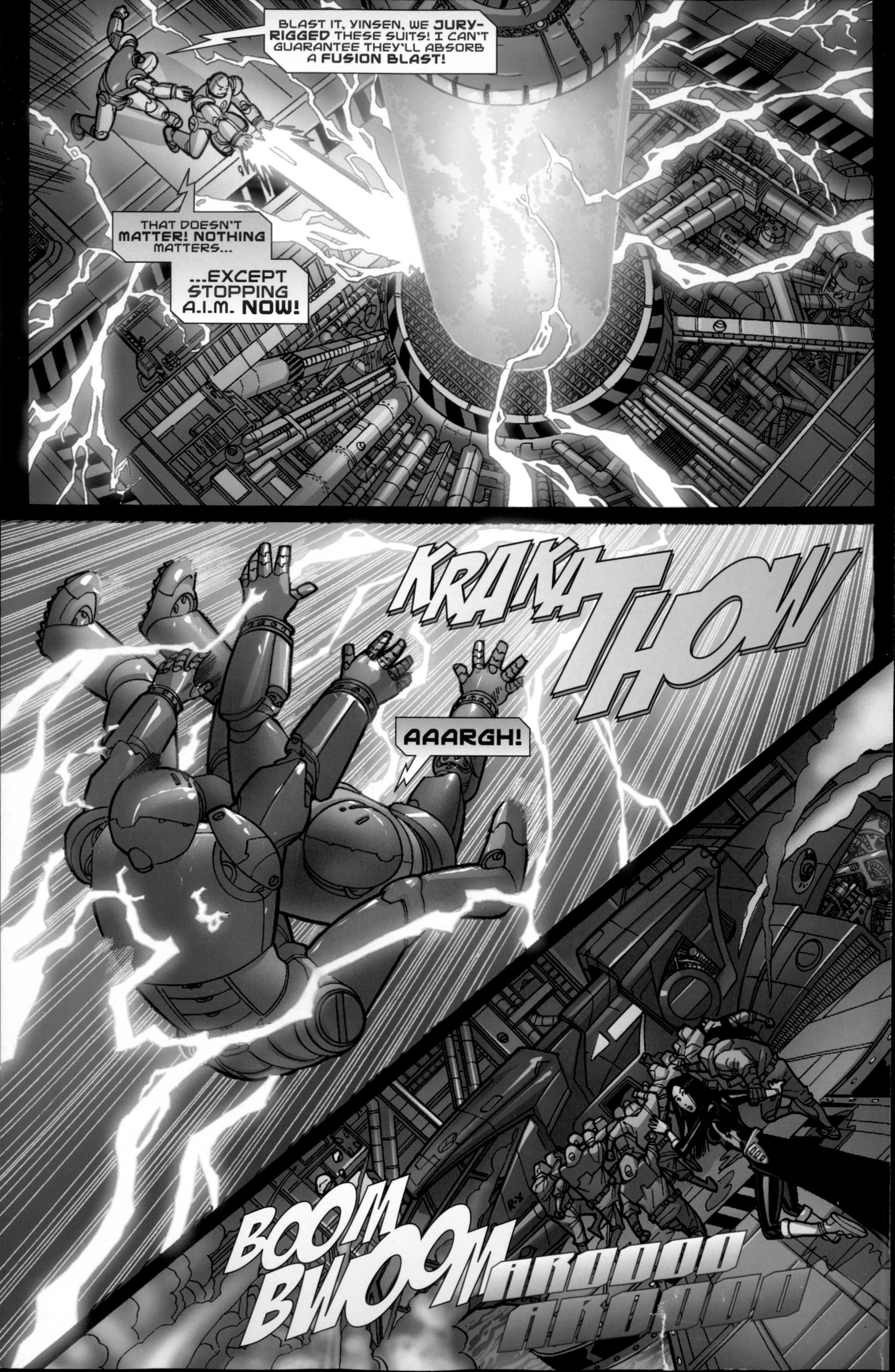

BLAST IT, YINSEN, WE JURY-RIGGED THESE SUITS! I CAN'T GUARANTEE THEY'LL ABSORB A FUSION BLAST!
THAT DOESN'T MATTER! NOTHING MATTERS...
...EXCEPT STOPPING A.I.M. NOW!
KRAKATHOW
AAARGH!
BOOM
BWOOM
AROOOO
AROOOO

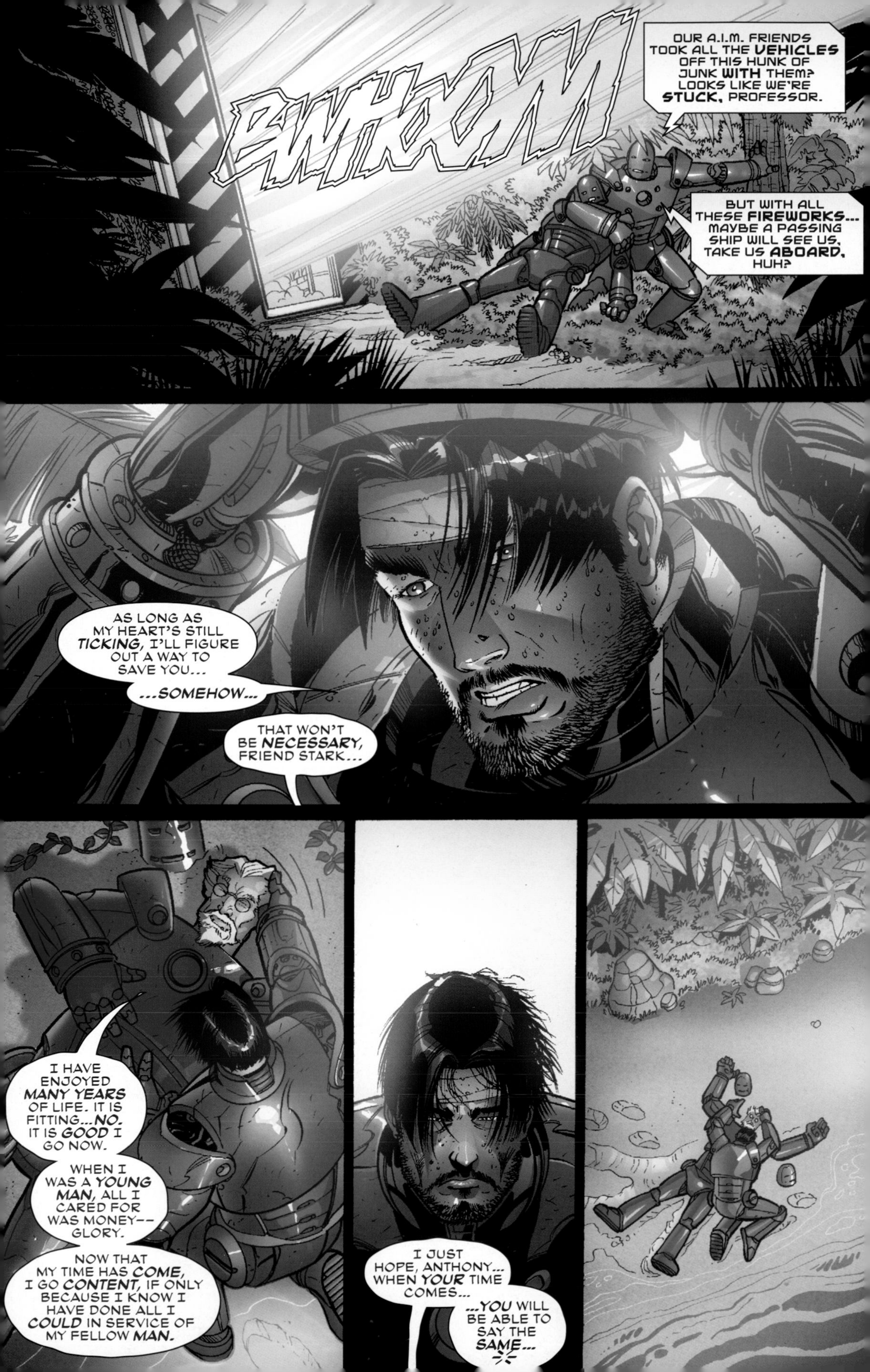

BWHOOM
OUR A.I.M. FRIENDS TOOK ALL THE VEHICLES OFF THIS HUNK OF JUNK WITH THEM? LOOKS LIKE WE'RE STUCK, PROFESSOR.
BUT WITH ALL THESE FIREWORKS... MAYBE A PASSING SHIP WILL SEE US, TAKE US ABOARD, HUH?
AS LONG AS MY HEART'S STILL TICKING, I'LL FIGURE OUT A WAY TO SAVE YOU...
...SOMEHOW...
THAT WON'T BE NECESSARY, FRIEND STARK...
I HAVE ENJOYED MANY YEARS OF LIFE. IT IS FITTING...NO. IT IS GOOD I GO NOW.
WHEN I WAS A YOUNG MAN, ALL I CARED FOR WAS MONEY-- GLORY.
NOW THAT MY TIME HAS COME, I GO CONTENT, IF ONLY BECAUSE I KNOW I HAVE DONE ALL I COULD IN SERVICE OF MY FELLOW MAN.
I JUST HOPE, ANTHONY... WHEN YOUR TIME COMES...
...YOU WILL BE ABLE TO SAY THE SAME...

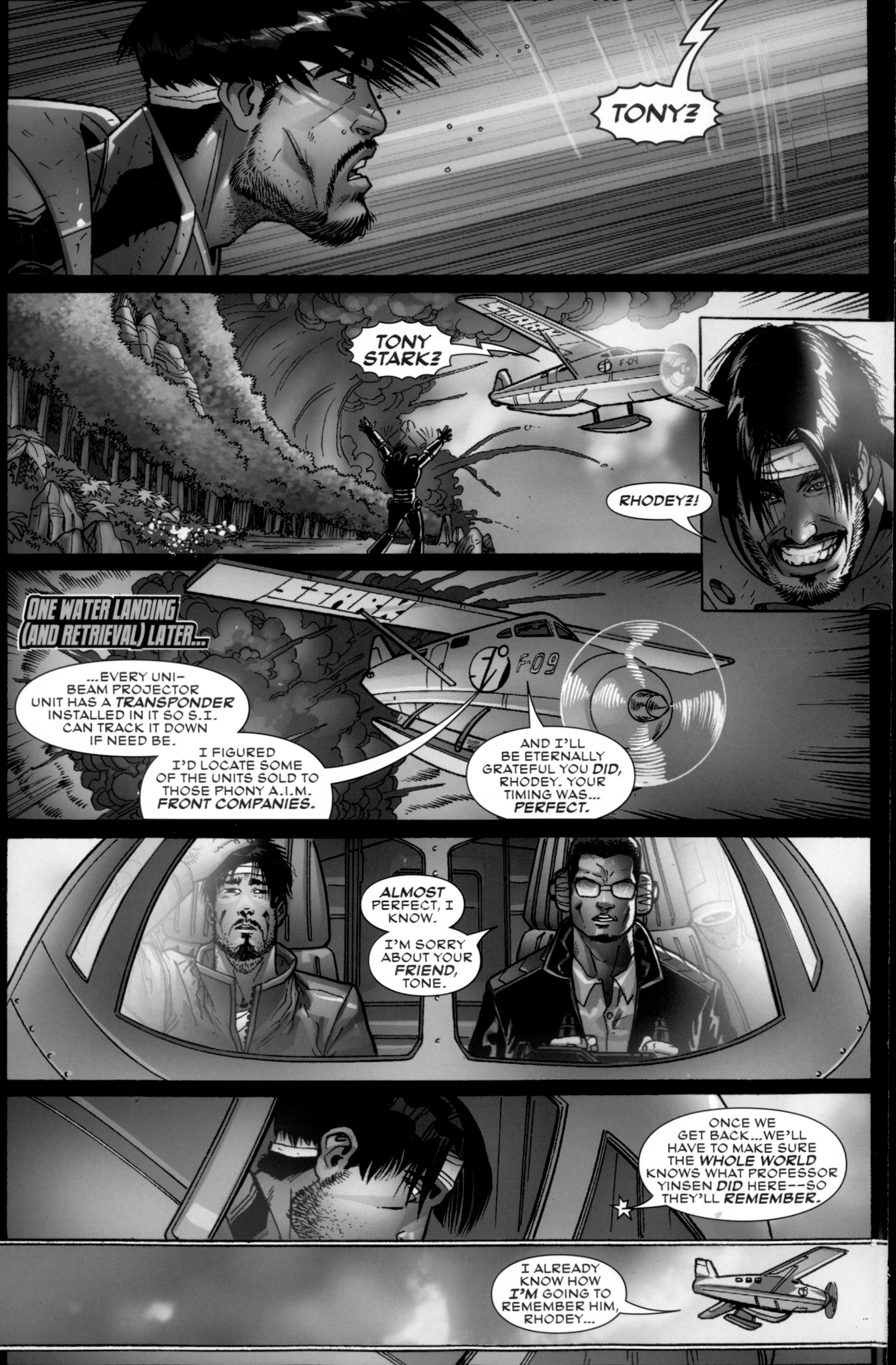
TONY?
TONY STARK?
RHODEY?!
ONE WATER LANDING (AND RETRIEVAL) LATER...
...EVERY UNI-BEAM PROJECTOR UNIT HAS A TRANSPONDER INSTALLED IN IT SO S.I. CAN TRACK IT DOWN IF NEED BE.
I FIGURED I'D LOCATE SOME OF THE UNITS SOLD TO THOSE PHONY A.I.M. FRONT COMPANIES.
AND I'LL BE ETERNALLY GRATEFUL YOU DID, RHODEY. YOUR TIMING WAS... PERFECT.
ALMOST PERFECT, I KNOW.
I'M SORRY ABOUT YOUR FRIEND, TONE.
ONCE WE GET BACK...WE'LL HAVE TO MAKE SURE THE WHOLE WORLD KNOWS WHAT PROFESSOR YINSEN DID HERE--SO THEY'LL REMEMBER.
I ALREADY KNOW HOW I'M GOING TO REMEMBER HIM, RHODEY...

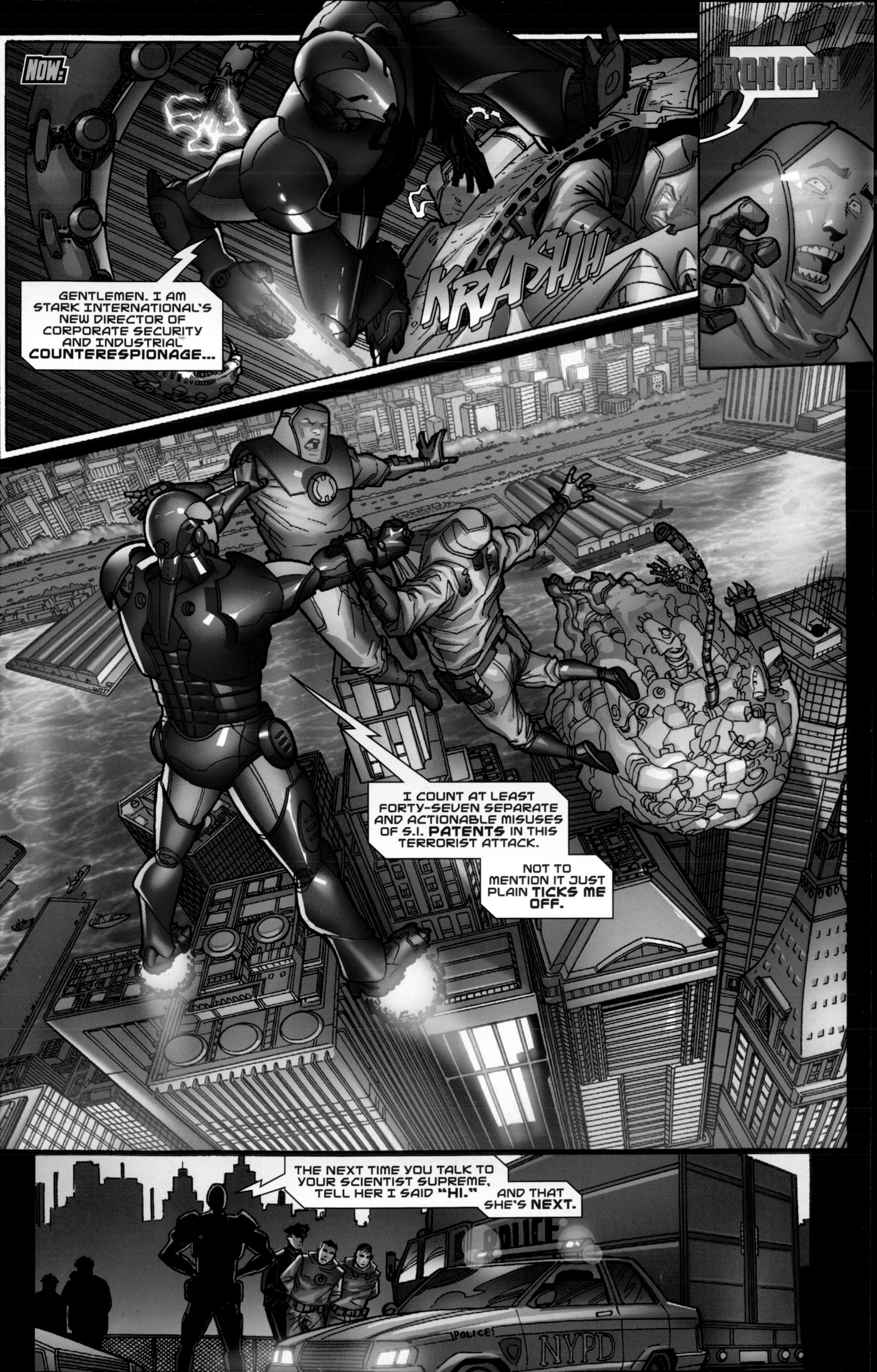
NOW:
IRON MAN
KRASHH
GENTLEMEN. I AM STARK INTERNATIONAL'S NEW DIRECTOR OF CORPORATE SECURITY AND INDUSTRIAL COUNTERESPIONAGE...
I COUNT AT LEAST FORTY-SEVEN SEPARATE AND ACTIONABLE MISUSES OF S.I. PATENTS IN THIS TERRORIST ATTACK.
NOT TO MENTION IT JUST PLAIN TICKS ME OFF.
THE NEXT TIME YOU TALK TO YOUR SCIENTIST SUPREME, TELL HER I SAID "HI."
AND THAT SHE'S NEXT.
POLICE
POLICE
NYPD

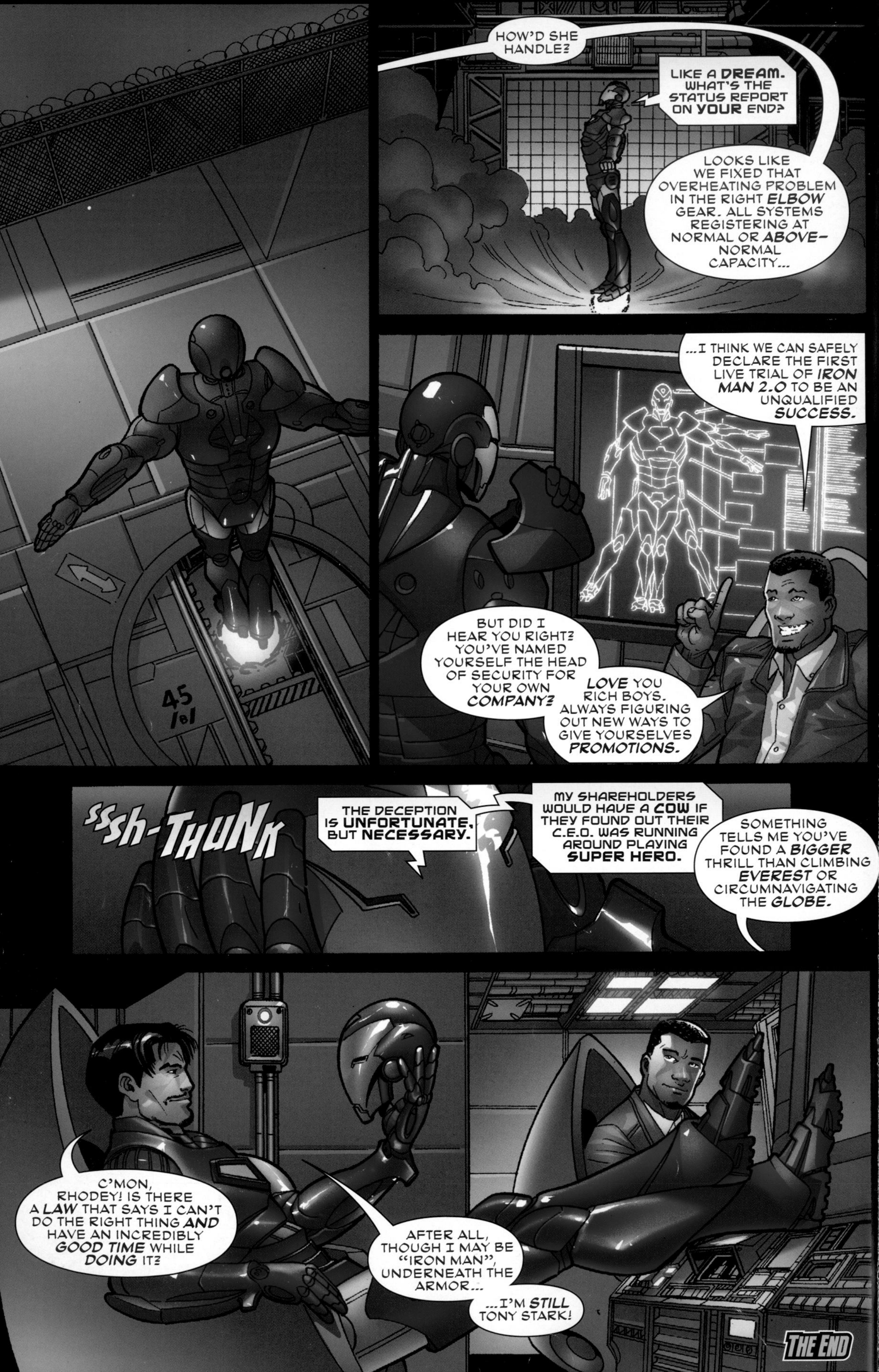
HOW'D SHE HANDLE?
LIKE A DREAM. WHAT'S THE STATUS REPORT ON YOUR END?
LOOKS LIKE WE FIXED THAT OVERHEATING PROBLEM IN THE RIGHT ELBOW GEAR. ALL SYSTEMS REGISTERING AT NORMAL OR ABOVE-NORMAL CAPACITY...
...I THINK WE CAN SAFELY DECLARE THE FIRST LIVE TRIAL OF IRON MAN 2.0 TO BE AN UNQUALIFIED SUCCESS.
BUT DID I HEAR YOU RIGHT? YOU'VE NAMED YOURSELF THE HEAD OF SECURITY FOR YOUR OWN COMPANY?
LOVE YOU RICH BOYS. ALWAYS FIGURING OUT NEW WAYS TO GIVE YOURSELVES PROMOTIONS.
45
/B/
SSSH-THUNK
THE DECEPTION IS UNFORTUNATE, BUT NECESSARY.
MY SHAREHOLDERS WOULD HAVE A COW IF THEY FOUND OUT THEIR C.E.O. WAS RUNNING AROUND PLAYING SUPER HERO.
SOMETHING TELLS ME YOU'VE FOUND A BIGGER THRILL THAN CLIMBING EVEREST OR CIRCUMNAVIGATING THE GLOBE.
C'MON, RHODEY! IS THERE A LAW THAT SAYS I CAN'T DO THE RIGHT THING AND HAVE AN INCREDIBLY GOOD TIME WHILE DOING IT?
AFTER ALL, THOUGH I MAY BE "IRON MAN", UNDERNEATH THE ARMOR...
...I'M STILL TONY STARK!
THE END